This book belongs to:

WITHDRAWN
FROM
STOCK

Contents

First published 2008 by Brown Watson
The Old Mill, 76 Fleckney Road,
Kibworth Beauchamp, Leic LE8 0HG

ISBN: 978 0 7097 1804 8
© 2008 Brown Watson, England
Reprinted 2008, 2009, 2010 (twice), 2012
Printed in Malaysia

EARLY READERS

Three Read Aloud Stories

Stories by Gill Davies

Illustrations by:
Gill Guile, Stephen Holmes,
Jane Swift and Lawrie Taylor

Brown Watson
ENGLAND

TIGER THINKS HARD

Tiger sits.

He sits and he thinks.

He sits and he thinks hard and he looks all around him.

Then he says:
"Oh, I am such an ordinary little tiger. I wish that I had pretty spots like you, Snake. I wish that I was tall like you, Giraffe. I wish that I could run as fast as you, Zebra."

Snake slides up the tree.

Tiger says, "Oh you are lucky, Snake. I wish I could go to the top of a tree and look at the sky from up there."

"But you are lucky too, Tiger," says Zebra: "You can roar. You can run on your four fast legs and you have nice black stripes – just like me!"

Then two little frogs talk
to Tiger.

"You are so lucky," the frogs
say to him. "You are so big.
You are so much bigger than
we are."

"I am," says Tiger. Tiger thinks
hard and then he says, "Yes, I
am very lucky to be me."

"We are all very lucky to be
us," hisses wise
Snake. "And yet
none of us are
the same."

KEY WORDS

a	sits
am	talk
black	than
he	that
him	thinks
like	wish
same	you
says	your

WHAT CAN YOU SEE HERE?

flowers

giraffe

zebra

tiger

snake

CHEERING UP LOLLIPOP

Father Bear tells Teddy that Lollipop Bear has a sore head today and cannot come over to play.

"Perhaps she will feel better soon," says Teddy. "Please may I take her something to cheer her up?"

"Yes," says Mother Bear. "That is a very good idea. Let's see what we can find."

The bears set off with lots of nice things in a cart. They have bread and jam and cakes.

"Hello," say some rabbits. "Where are you going?"

"To see Lollipop," Teddy tells them. "She has a bad head. We want to cheer her up."

"We can give her a nice sweet lettuce," say the rabbits. "Here you are!"

Now all the bears are at the house. Lollipop is outside. She smiles.

"I could hear you all coming down the road," she says. "So I have come out to see you."

Teddy shows her all the good things in the cart.

"How wonderful," says Lollipop. "I was feeling much better already but now I feel even better still."

KEY WORDS

all	let's
bad	lots
cakes	Mother
could	nice
Father	please
feel	something
good	teddy
head	things

WHAT CAN YOU SEE HERE?

rabbits

squirrels

house

cat

cart

HOME SWEET HOME

Anna and Harry want to play in the old caravan.

"This will make a great den," says Harry.

But Mummy tells them they can't play there.

"No," she says. "That caravan is very old. It might fall over. It is not a safe place to play at all."

So Anna and Harry play with a ball instead.

That night the wind blows. It blows so hard that the hen house falls down.

In the morning the hens are nowhere to be seen. Anna and Harry look everywhere.
"Hello, hens," they call. "Where are you? The wind has stopped now. Please come back."

Then Anna and Harry hear Dad calling to them. "Come and see what I have found."

"Here are all the hens," says Dad. "Safe in the old caravan."

"But Mum says the caravan is not a safe place," cries Harry.

"Safe enough for hens," laughs Dad. "They are not big and heavy and they don't jump about like you two do."

So the hens stay snug in the caravan while Dad mends their old hen house.

KEY WORDS

be	jump
but	morning
call	night
down	not
everywhere	place
hello	play
hens	this
house	want

WHAT CAN YOU SEE HERE?

fence

wheel

caravan

hen house

hen